CHRISTMAS

ALEXA TEWKESBURY

CWR

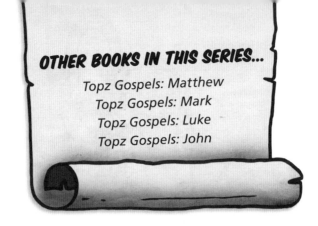

OTHER BOOKS IN THIS SERIES...

Topz Gospels: Matthew
Topz Gospels: Mark
Topz Gospels: Luke
Topz Gospels: John

Introduction by Danny

Do you know the Christmas story? Have you heard about Mary and Joseph, and the shepherds and the angels? What about the three wise men who followed a star to find a king? Or the cruel King Herod, who threw an epic tantrum because the only king he was interested in was himself?

And has anyone ever told you how Jesus, God's Son, was born in a mucky stable because there was nowhere else for His mum, Mary, to go? And how Mary tucked Him up for His first sleep (wait for it) in an animals' feeding trough?!

You see, all those things – that's what Christmas is. **IT'S JESUS' BIRTHDAY** – Jesus coming to earth to live with us and grow up with us, and teach us all about Father God.

3

It's the unfolding of God's action plan to make us His friends again, so that one day we can all live with God forever. Wow!

When I read about Christmas in the Bible, it becomes so real to me and I get so excited that I can see it all in my head – the people, the angels, the star (I'm crazy about stars!), and especially the baby!

In fact, when I *really* think about it – really let myself sink into the story – it's almost as if I'm there. Right there. Watching and listening, and being part of that very first Christmas…

CHAPTER 1
Stars
(Isaiah 40 v 26)

'WHAT ARE YOU DOING?'

John steps out from a huddle of trees into the moonlight. He wrinkles his nose and stares at the boy in front of him.

'Danny, are you all right?' He asks again: 'What are you doing?'

Danny stands on tiptoe on a flat-topped mound of rock. His arms reach upwards. His fingers stretch out as if trying to grasp something. He doesn't move, and he doesn't reply.

John's small brown dog, Gruff, trots out of the shadows. Gruff takes no notice of the boy on the rock. He just explores the ground with his nose, snuffling in the dust.

John shakes his head. 'Sometimes you are a bit weird, Danny, do you know that? I don't know what you think you're up to but you look... daft.'

Danny grunts. His shoulders slump. He drops his arms. 'Ugh. You've spoilt it now.'

'Spoilt what?'

'What I was doing.'

'But what *are* you doing?' John says. 'You're standing on a random rock, looking weird! And we're supposed to be collecting firewood.'

Danny folds his arms. 'If you must know, I was seeing what it would feel like to reach for a star.' He says it as if it's obvious.

'*What?*'

'Don't laugh at me,' says Danny. 'I was imagining what it would feel like to grab hold of one – to have it in my hands and pull it towards me. Haven't you ever done that? I mean, don't you ever wonder what it would be like to hold a star?'

'Uh... no.' John's nose wrinkles again.

'Well, why not?' Danny says. 'I love stars. Look at them, all over the sky! And this bit of sky that we can see – it's only a tiny little fraction of the whole thing. There are hundreds of stars out there – thousands. Millions. Wouldn't you like to be able to touch just one?'

'I don't know,' John shrugs. 'Never thought about it. Anyway, I hate to point this out, but somehow I don't think anyone ever reached a star by standing on a rock.'

Danny shivers. He ties the belt of his tunic a little tighter around his waist. 'Yeah, well, maybe that's because no one's ever tried hard enough. **STARS ARE INCREDIBLE.**'

He jumps down from his reaching point and marches towards the trees. 'Come on, then, hurry up. We've got firewood to find.'

Danny glances back, and stops. A smile brightens his face.

Now it's John who stands on the rock. He doesn't reach out, but his head is tilted upwards and he stares into the night sky.

'You've got a point, Danny,' John says. 'They are pretty incredible. All those stars… just millions of them. They're amazing.'

'Yup,' answers Danny. His eyes sweep once more across the blue-black arc overhead. 'Let's get that wood,' he says. 'I don't know about you, but I'm freezing.'

'You know stars are a lot bigger than they look, right?' John hops down from the rock and follows his friend. 'They only look tiny because they're so far away. Miles. Thousands of miles! I mean, you'd need really big hands to hold a star. *Really* big.'

Danny laughs. 'Yep! Biggest hands ever in the whole history of big hands!' He peers down, spots a couple of sticks and stoops to pick them up. 'Yeah, thanks, John, but I did know that.'

'And anyway, you'd never be able to even touch one,' adds John. 'They're really hot. Burning hot.'

'Yeah, I sort of knew that, too.'

John nods. They both scan the ground for more wood.

'Tell you what, though,' John says, 'you've got plenty of time to keep trying because stars can last a massively long time. Years and years. A lot more years than we can.'

Danny glances at him. 'I know. I do know about stars, John.'

'Oh.'

'Do you know what I wish, though?'

'What?'

'I wish we'd looked for firewood before it got so dark. I can't see a thing.'

John sighs. 'Me neither.'

The moon is clear and bright, but new and just a tiny crescent, like the white part of a fingernail. It doesn't shed much light.

'Can't you train Gruff to fetch wood?' Danny asks. 'I bet he can see better in the dark than we can.'

'Gruff fetches sticks, don't you, Gruff?' John crouches to ruffle the fur on the small dog's head.

'Yeah, but only when you throw them for him, which means having some to throw in the first place! And we don't have any! Anyway, here.' Danny laughs and hands John one of the two sticks he's managed to find. 'Take it,' he says. 'That's one each… that'll have to do. Let's get back to camp.'

CHAPTER 2
Mary
(Isaiah 40 v 5)

Something clatters into the dust beside Danny's head. He jolts awake.

'What…?'

There's a second clatter next to John.

'What's that? What's happening?' John squints upwards from his makeshift bed on the ground.

Sarah stands over him, arms folded, lips pressed tight together in disapproval.

Josie stares down at Danny, her face dim with the same expression.

Danny rolls over. He sees a pile of wood beside him. John has spotted the small heap next to him, too.

'Did you just…?' Danny props himself up on his elbows. 'Josie, did you just nearly drop a load of wood on my head?'

Josie shrugs. 'Did you two just keep us awake half the night moaning about the cold?'

'It *was* cold. It still is.'

'You're telling me.' John curls into a ball and pulls his thin blanket up over his chin.

'Yes, John.' Sarah picks up a long stick from the pile at her feet and prods him. 'That's why you and Danny were supposed to come back to camp with wood. Lots of wood. So we could keep the fire going longer.'

'Not our fault we couldn't find any.'

'How could you not find any?! Josie and me – we've only been up since it got light and look at all the sticks we've found already!'

'The ones you nearly dropped on our heads, you mean?'

Sarah ignores him. 'What exactly were you doing all that time? You were gone ages.'

'Well, we were walking Gruff and…'

'Actually, I really don't need to know.' Sarah squats down. She scoops up an armful of wood and plonks it onto the heap of cold ash from yesterday evening's fire. 'I'm off to Nazareth. We need bread. Who's coming with me?'

'Bread?' Benny flicks back his blanket. 'Me – I'm absolutely ready!'

Josie raises her eyebrows. 'Ready? Don't you want to have a wash first?'

'Nah.' Benny makes a face. 'Too cold for washing.'

'I'll come,' says Paul.

'Me, too,' says Danny.

'And me.' Dave clambers upright. He yawns and stretches.

'John?' Danny looks at his friend.

Gruff still lies asleep at John's feet. Saucy, Sarah's cat is curled up beside him. Her nose is hidden in the cluster of her paws, as if she's trying to keep it warm.

'Think I'll give it a miss,' John grunts.

'Good,' says Sarah. 'While we're gone, you can get the fire going…'

Nazareth is close. It doesn't take the Gang long to walk there – no more than 15 minutes. They slip together through the narrow streets lined with pale, square buildings. The smell of fresh-baked bread reaches them before they even arrive at the market.

'I love that bread smell,' says Benny. 'It's so… warm.'

'How can something smell warm?' Danny asks.

'I dunno, but bread does. Even when it's cold.'

It's still early but the market is already busy. Some people selling, others buying. Voices rise and fall; footsteps shuffle and scurry.

Josie watches the movement. 'I love the market. I wish we could have a stall here.'

'Selling what?' Danny asks.

'I don't know. I don't mind, really. Anything. I'd just love to be a market seller.'

Benny shakes his head. 'I'd have to sell *things*. You know, cloth or baskets or something. I couldn't sell food. If it was food I'd baked or grown – I couldn't bear to part with it.'

Danny stops. He watches a man outside a low building work a piece of wood with different tools. The man shapes it, carves it, stands back every now and again to study it, then works on it some more.

'I don't know about having a market stall,' Danny says, 'but I wish I could do what Joseph does. Whenever we come here, he's always busy making something. He's so good at it.'

Sarah giggles.

Danny looks at her, confused by her laughter. 'Well, he is.'

'It's not that.'

'What then?'

'It's just…' Sarah bites her lip in a grin. Her eyes flick from one to another of her friends. 'It's just, I know something none of you do.'

Josie frowns. 'What? What do you know? And why

don't *I* know? We tell each other everything.'

'It's supposed to be a secret.'

'What is?' demands Josie, playfully.

'The *thing*.' Sarah's face flushes with excitement. 'I overheard him – Joseph – saying that he'd finally asked and it was happening. But he said it had to be a secret till the end of the week when he was going to announce it to everyone.'

Josie still looks a little annoyed. 'Everyone who?'

'I don't know,' Sarah shrugs her shoulders. 'Family, maybe? Just everyone.'

Paul blinks. 'Is it me or is this getting really complicated?'

'What on earth are you on about?' Josie stares hard at Sarah, who sneaks a glance at Joseph. 'Well… Oh, I suppose it must be all right to say something. I mean, it is the end of the week now and I've been dying to tell someone…' She lowers her voice even so. 'You know Mary?'

Paul blinks again and shakes his head in confusion. 'I thought this was about Joseph.'

Sarah raises her eyes. 'Yeah, it is, but you know *Mary*?' she repeats.

'Of course we know Mary!' Josie snaps.

'So, the thing is… ' Once again, Sarah's eyes dance from friend to friend. 'Mary has just got engaged – to Joseph!'

'*What?*' Josie's mouth falls open.

'Yep – Mary and Joseph – **THEY'RE GOING TO BE MARRIED!**'

CHAPTER 3

Flash!*

(Isaiah 9 v 2)

Mary's house gleams under the morning sun. Its shadow flows outwards from its walls, a blue-grey pool across the dusty street. Different-sized stone jars stand in a cluster near the front door. A smell of baking drifts through the windows.

The Gang sit on the ground at the corner of the road and Benny's nostrils twitch.

'Mary does a lot of baking,' he says. 'I'm sure I can smell cooking almost every time I walk past her house.'

Sarah's eyes sparkle. 'I'd love to ask her how she feels – I can't even imagine it. There you are, getting on with your normal day, and then out of the blue, someone asks you to marry them, and everything's different! She must feel like a brand-new person.'

'Do you reckon he got down on one knee?' asks Josie with a smile. 'It's so romantic, isn't it?'

Danny snorts. 'No, it's not! People get married all the time. It's not romantic, it's just what they do.'

'I think it's a bit romantic,' says Paul. 'He wouldn't ask her if he didn't love her. And people are all smiley at weddings, all gooey and all, "Ooh, look at the bride – isn't she beautiful!"' he says in a sing-song voice.

Sarah suddenly holds up her hand. 'Shush a minute. There's Mary.'

A young woman – very young, not many years older than the Gang – steps outside the house. She rubs her hands together as if brushing something from them, probably flour, and stoops to pick up one of the stone jars by the door. But she hesitates.

Perhaps it's the warm feel of the sun on her back – or perhaps the sky is such a dazzling clear-blue that she can't resist snatching a few moments to gaze into it – but she straightens. She lifts her head and lets her eyes sweep the cloudless space above her. Then she closes them, and turns her face towards the sun.

Even from where they sit at the end of the road, the Gang can see her smile.

Sarah nudges Josie. 'Look how happy she is. It *is* romantic. I think it's lovely.'

Mary turns back to the jars. With both hands, she picks one up and carries it into the house.

'Shall we say something to her?' says Dave. 'You know – congratulations? It's what you do, isn't it, when someone's getting married.'

Sarah shakes her head. 'I'm not really sure if anyone's supposed to know yet. Anyway, we should probably get back to John.'

She begins to turn.

A bright white light suddenly fills her vision. A dazzling flash! Sarah freezes and throws up her hands to protect her eyes.

'Ow!' Benny yelps. His hands are in front of his face too.

'What happened?' gasps Paul. 'Was that lightning? Is there a storm? What's going on?'

There's a crash. The sound of something shattering and splintering into pieces.

'It's not a storm, that wasn't thunder!' Danny's eyes are panicked, but he barely moves, and just stares down the street. 'I think… I think it came from inside Mary's house!'

There is no more noise. The light is no longer blinding, but there's a glow inside the house that radiates outwards through the window and gently melts the shadow on the ground – a glow stronger than sunlight.

'Mary!' Sarah gasps. **'SOMETHING'S HAPPENING TO MARY!'**

She runs, and the Gang follow after her. They kick up dust as their feet scamper on the road.

As she reaches the front of the house, Sarah stops. She glances back and puts a finger to her lips to make sure everyone stays quiet. Crouching down and barely moving, she peers through the window. Close behind, Danny copies her.

What they spot first is the stone jar Mary had been holding. She must have dropped it. It lies in jagged fragments on the floor.

Danny points to it and whispers, 'The crash!'

What they see next is Mary's face. Her eyes are wide and unblinking, and her mouth is open in disbelief. She stands completely still as if made of stone like the fractured jar, staring at something across the room. Is she even breathing?

Danny and Sarah, half afraid, trace the line of her gaze with their own. They suck in a breath. Without thinking, they hold on to it as if they've forgotten how to breathe, like Mary.

THEY CAN SEE IT TOO.

Against the far wall is a figure – the thing they could see glowing brightly through the window. The figure might be standing – or is it floating? Are its feet actually touching the floor?

It shines with brilliant light.

CHAPTER 4

Special

(Luke 1 v 26–38)

'What is it?'

Dave fidgets. From where he is, he can't see a thing. 'What's happening in there? What's going on?'

Mary hasn't moved. Even as the figure speaks, she stands frozen like a statue.

'Peace be with you, Mary.' The figure's voice is quiet. Gentle. 'God loves you very much. He wants you to know how special you are to Him. He is going to bless you more than you could ever believe possible.'

Mary's shoulders heave as she finally draws in a breath. 'But who are you?' Her voice is quieter than the figure's. Sarah and Danny have to strain to hear. 'What do you want?'

'My name is Gabriel.' The figure smiles. He sees the fear in Mary's eyes. He notices the anxious lines that appear between her brows.

'Don't be afraid, Mary. **I'M HERE BECAUSE I HAVE SOME NEWS FOR YOU.** Wonderful news. God has chosen you to do something very special. You're going to have a baby. A little boy. But not just any little boy. This child will be God's own Son. His *only* Son. And God wants you to be Jesus' mother.'

Mary shakes her head. Just a tiny movement at first, then bigger and stronger. How can this be?

'You are to call the baby Jesus,' says Gabriel. 'God will make Him King of His people. **JESUS WILL SAVE THEM, MARY. HE'LL SAVE THEM FROM ALL THE THINGS THEY'VE EVER DONE WRONG, SO THAT THEY CAN BE GOD'S FRIENDS – FOREVER.'**

Outside the window, Sarah's heart drums in her ears. She snatches a look at Danny. His face says everything she feels: this is the most incredible conversation they have ever heard! They should leave, shouldn't they? It's private… an extraordinary and private moment between Mary and God's messenger. Between Mary and God.

But how can they pull themselves away?

'What people?' Mary splutters. She stumbles forward. 'How can any of this happen? How? I can't give birth to a king – any king! I can't! I'm going to marry Joseph. Soon. How can I have a baby now?'

'It'll be all right.' Again, a smile warms Gabriel's face. 'God will send His Spirit to you. You will know His power.'

There is a moment of quiet before the angel speaks again. 'You remember Elizabeth, don't you?' Gabriel says.

Mary nods her head. 'She's one of my relatives. What about her?'

'Elizabeth is having a baby. She may be very old, but God has chosen her to have a special child too.'

The fear in Mary's eyes changes to puzzlement, then to wonder.

'You see, Mary,' says Gabriel, **'THERE IS NOTHING GOD CANNOT DO.'**

Mary stares. She blinks in the angel's radiant glow. Slowly, distractedly, she reaches out to draw up a stool. She sinks down. Her fingers twist together. She watches them twine into each other. Then she lets her hands drop into her lap.

'All right.' She lifts her eyes again towards Gabriel. 'Yes… I am God's servant. If this is what He wants, then let it happen.'

And as suddenly as he arrived, Gabriel is gone.

It's still daylight outside, but the room seems dark, and full of shadows without the brightness of his beaming light.

Mary stays where she is, perched on the stool, lost in her thoughts, the dimness and the silence.

CHAPTER 5

Questions

(Isaiah 9 v 6)

John kicks at the cold ash of the camp fire with a sandalled foot, listening to the Gang's excited chatter. Beside him are sticks – a precarious-looking pile of them. While the others have been out getting breakfast in Nazareth, he's been on a wood hunt. He's done well, too! The stack he's found should keep the fire burning for a few hours after dark. That'll save them from another chilly, sleepless night.

'That was an angel. No doubt about it! Gabriel is definitely an angel,' says Danny, through a mouthful of bread.

'I can't believe it,' answers Sarah. **'I CAN'T BELIEVE GOD SENT AN ANGEL TO TALK TO MARY AND WE WERE THERE TO SEE IT!'**

John clears his throat loudly. 'We weren't *all* there to see it. In case you've forgotten, I was stuck here – collecting firewood so you lot wouldn't get cold later.'

Josie throws him a sideways look. 'You could have come with us if you'd wanted to. Anyway, not all of us saw the angel.'

'Josie's right,' mumbles Benny, crumbs spilling out of his mouth. The piece of crust he's trying to chew is too big. 'We couldn't all get round the window. But, wow, did we see the light!'

'The light was blazing!' says Paul. 'And there was this flash – right in Mary's kitchen. Must have scared her to bits!'

'To *absolute* bits!' says Dave. 'It scared us, and we were safely outside! Even if an angel is sent from God, I think having one arrive out of the blue when you're in the middle of baking must be terrifying…'

John flops down beside him. He inspects the toes of his right foot sticking out from his sandals. They are powdered and speckled with ash. He flicks at it, trying to brush it off. There's a frown on his face.

'I wish you hadn't missed it, John.' Sarah crouches next to him. 'I wish you'd been there too. I really do. But don't be angry. We know something amazing now. Something we wouldn't know if we'd *all* missed it.'

John carries on staring at his ash-dusted toes.

Sarah gives him a nudge. 'God's chosen Mary to be the mother of His Son. His *only* Son. The only one He's ever going to have!'

Danny holds out some bread. John eyes it a moment, then takes it.

'Thanks,' he grunts. But his frown doesn't relax, and he doesn't eat. He just turns the bread over and over in his hands.

'What?' asks Danny.

John looks up at him. 'God – who created you, me,

everything – the whole entire universe – God, who's more powerful than we'll ever be able to understand – God, who even knows how many of those stars you love so much are in the sky because He put them there – are you telling me that His Son is going to be born here, on the earth? Are you seriously saying God's Son is going to live here with everyone as a… human being?'

Danny shrugs. 'I know it's hard to believe because you weren't there. But it's not what *we're* saying, John. It's what God's saying.'

John shakes his head. It isn't hard to believe just because he wasn't there. It would be hard to grasp even if he'd heard it for himself.

'You said the angel told Mary that this baby, Jesus, would save people so they could be friends with God again,' he says. 'But how? How's He going to do that?'

Saucy, who has been investigating the base of the wood pile, suddenly leaps forward and lands about a third of the way up its wobbly slope. The sticks immediately collapse underneath her, so she leaps again in search of a firmer landing. She doesn't find one. As her feet make contact with the heap again, her weight and the instability of the stack create a mini avalanche. Spooked by the collapse and clatter, the little cat does another sideways jump, into Sarah's arms.

Sarah laughs.

It takes a moment, but John's frown disappears. He repeats his question. 'How's this Jesus going to save everyone? How, Danny?'

This time it's Danny who shakes his head. 'I don't know. But He will. **IF THAT'S GOD'S PLAN, THEN THAT'S WHAT WILL HAPPEN.'**

He lifts his eyes; gazes up into the sky. A few rags of cloud drift by above them. So slowly as to hardly move at all. They gleam white in the sunlight against the sharp, bright blue.

'What do you think, though?' Danny says. 'When Jesus grows up and stands on a rock – do you suppose He'll be able to touch the stars?'

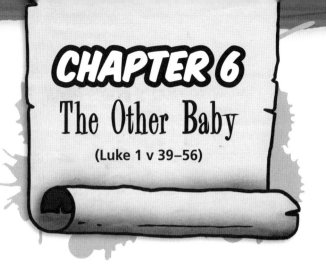

CHAPTER 6
The Other Baby
(Luke 1 v 39–56)

'How much further?'

Benny groans. He crouches down to massage the backs of his sore feet where they rub against his sandals.

'Dunno,' replies Josie. 'But we can't be far away, can we? We've been walking for ages.'

Mary is on her way to visit Elizabeth and her husband, Zechariah, and the Gang have followed her all the way from Nazareth. Sarah wants to stay close by to keep an eye out for Mary and make sure she's safe. But Benny keeps stopping, and they've lost sight of her. They don't know how far ahead she is. They don't even know where Elizabeth lives, so they can't be sure they'll find her again.

'Oh, come on, Benny!' says Sarah. She sounds faintly annoyed. 'How can Mary walk so much faster than us? We need to catch up. What if something's happened to her?'

'Like what?' says Dave.

'I don't know.' Sarah chews at her thumbnail. With her other hand, she fiddles with Saucy's ears. Saucy doesn't

27

seem to mind. Tucked snuggly into a leather bag slung across Sarah's shoulders, just her head peeps out. 'I'm worried about her. It's a long way for her to walk on her own, and she's having a baby.'

'Not yet, she isn't. Not for a few months.' Danny is slightly ahead of the others. 'She'll be fine, she's used to walking. Like you say, Sarah, she's having a baby, she's not ill.'

Saucy gives a sharp shake of her head. Sarah glances down at her, half surprised, as if she hasn't noticed she's been playing with her ears. She smoothes the fur on top of the little cat's head.

'I know,' she says. 'It's just that we've walked all this way to make sure she's safe, and now we've lost her.'

Benny still rubs his sore feet. 'Don't blame me. It's not my fault these sandals don't fit.'

Danny reaches the brow of the hill. The track they've been following trickles steeply down the other side. There are a few thin-looking trees scattered on the slope and some low, scrubby bushes. And, further away, almost to the horizon, he sees houses: squat and blocky and clustered together. This must be the town where Elizabeth and Zechariah live!

He waits for the others to catch up. Then he stretches out an arm and points to a familiar figure in the distance.

'Oh, Mary's fine, by the way, Sarah,' he says. 'See?'

Perhaps Mary has stopped for a rest or a drink of water. Perhaps she just wants a moment to enjoy the sun and gaze at the spectacular views of the hills – but for whatever reason, Topz have caught up with her, and Sarah is relieved that they have sight of her again.

*   *   *

Danny sits on a tuft of grass high up on a hill slope while Benny, Paul, Dave and Josie are camped some way below. He's aware of the vague flicker of orange from the fire they've started. His friends' voices rise towards him now and again on a light breeze. Otherwise there's silence.

Overhead, the sky is patched with cloud; deep black against the darkening blue of the evening sky. As the clouds drift, a sliver of moon peeps out, before being covered again by the shadowy, travelling tufts. Patches of sky reveal the pinheads of stars. They glisten and sparkle, and Danny's eyes dance from one to the next, to the next.

'FATHER GOD, WHY AM I SO EXCITED?'

Danny's lips move just slightly as he begins his whispered prayer.

Ever since the angel visited Mary, I'm sure my heart's been beating twice as fast as it used to. All the time. Even when I wake up in the middle of the night, or first thing in the morning, the only thought in my head is that we've got caught up in something… amazing! More than amazing – incredible, unbelievable, STUPENDOUS… 'Stonking,' Benny would say, but I don't even think that's enough to describe it.

You're doing something, God. Something You've been planning. Something You've always known You were going to do. From the beginning of time… You're reaching out to the earth. To all the people You've made. All the people You love – everyone. No matter who they are, or what they've done. No matter if they're rich or poor, whether they think they're important or the least important person who ever lived. You're holding out Your huge, caring arms. It's as if You want to scoop us all up in an enormous hug. Only the hug isn't with Your arms. The hug isn't You, folding Yourself around us, wrapping us up.

The hug is a baby: Jesus.

You're giving us Your Son, to come and live with us here in the world. You're giving us Your Son so that we can get to know You by getting to know Him. He's the one who will show us how to be Your friends.

You're giving us Your Son because of how much You love us.

Elizabeth knows how special Jesus is – how special Mary is too, because You've chosen Mary to be His mum! When Mary arrived at Elizabeth's house, Elizabeth called her 'the most blessed of all women'. She said that as soon as she heard Mary call out hello, her own baby, who won't even be born for another three months, jumped inside her! Her own baby knew the voice was Mary's – and knew Mary is going to be the mother of Jesus.

But that's right, isn't it? That's exactly what would happen. Because You've given Elizabeth her baby, too. Elizabeth may be old – way too old to have a baby – but when You decide to work a miracle, nothing can stop it. So now, there will be two miracle babies.

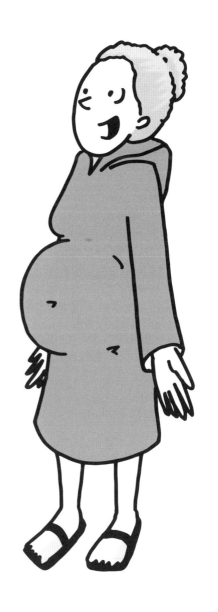

And I know, I just know, that they're going to be really important to each other.

Mary prayed a prayer to You. A prayer of praise. She spoke it out. She just about burst with energy and enthusiasm. She loves You, God, so much. I don't think I've ever heard anyone praise You quite like that before. I want to remember the words. I want to remember the way Mary said them. So that I can praise You like that too...

'My heart praises the Lord; my soul is glad because of God my Saviour, for he has remembered me... From now on all people will call me happy, because of the great things the Mighty God has done for me. His name is holy.'

You've remembered all of us, God. Every single one. One day, You want us all to live with You in heaven. You're sending Jesus to make that happen.

I've never felt like this before. If I'm this excited now, when Jesus hasn't even been born yet, imagine what I'll be like when He actually arrives!

Thank You, God – from the bottom of my thumping heart.

CHAPTER 7
John, the Messenger
(Luke 1 v 57–79)

'Danny! Benny!' Dave is bright red in the face. He's been running – all the way from the market in Nazareth to the river.

Benny and Danny are playing leapfrog in the shallow water at the river's edge. Benny is bent over, head tucked in, braced to take his friend's weight. Danny splashes at speed towards him.

'Benny! Danny!'

Benny hears Dave's call. He turns his face in the direction of the shout. He lifts his head. Dave tears towards him, flapping his arms to attract his and Danny's attention.

Danny is focused for a moment on his leap. As Benny's head goes up, his hands are already launching towards the flattish mound of Benny's back. His legs kick out ready to clear it, but not far enough. Mid-air, he catches the side of Benny's back with his foot. Benny, taken by surprise, loses his balance, and Danny's momentum is lost too. They topple, one heaped upon the other, into the water.

'What did you do that for?' Danny scrambles to his feet. He tries to brush the river water from his face but his hands are wet too. So is his tunic. Soaked through!

'It's not my fault,' grumbles Benny. He stands slowly, pushing back his dripping hair. 'It's Dave. Didn't you hear him yelling? I got distracted.'

'Benny! Danny!' Dave has reached the riverbank. Out of breath, he leans forward and rests his hands on his knees.

'Anyway' – Benny ignores him – 'that was totally your fault, Danny. Why didn't you stop?'

'I couldn't, could I? I was mid-air.'

'You *could* have stopped,' Benny argues. 'I bet *I* could have stopped.'

'I bet you couldn't.'

'I so could!'

'Couldn't.'

'Yeah, Danny, I really could.'

'Hey!' Dave stands on the bank, upright now, hands on his hips and a frown digging a furrow into his forehead.

A pair of dripping faces turn towards him.

Dave looks from one to the other. 'Do you two want to hear my news, or not?'

'I hope it's *good* news,' Benny grunts.

'Yeah.' Danny leans his head towards one shoulder and waggles a finger in his ear to get out the water. 'News worth getting soaked for.'

Dave grins. 'Mary's back.'

'Back in Nazareth?' Danny jerks his head up.

'Yup. John and Sarah are back here too.'

John and Sarah have been away. When the rest of the

Gang returned to their camp outside Nazareth, they'd stayed on in the hill country with Mary. Sarah didn't want to leave her.

'Seriously, Sarah,' John had moaned, 'you are such a fusspot.'

But he'd agreed to stay with her anyway.

The grin on Dave's face stretches wider. 'And that's not all.'

Benny blinks at him. Drops of water from his fringe dribble into his eyes. 'What?'

Dave can't keep it to himself any longer.

'ELIZABETH'S HAD HER BABY.'

* * *

Sarah and Josie stare into the glow of the small fire Danny and Benny have made. The days and nights are warmer now – it's later in the year and they don't need a fire to chase away the cold. But Benny and Danny stand over it, using the heat to dry off their tunics.

'Everyone's talking about Elizabeth's baby,' says John. 'They all know – and I don't mean just friends and relations, I mean *everyone*. People who live near, and people who live miles away.'

'It's all over the market in Nazareth too,' says Josie.

Sarah smiles. 'That's because people know God's behind it. They know Elizabeth's baby is full of Him.'

Danny shakes the folds of his tunic in the warm air rising from the fire, hoping to help it dry more quickly.

Paul scratches in the dust with a stone. He writes

the names 'Mary' and 'Elizabeth'. He wants to write Zechariah's name too, but he isn't sure how to spell it. He doesn't understand what's happened. He wonders, if he writes down the names, reads them over, pictures each person, maybe it will all start to make sense to him.

'I don't get it,' says Benny. 'It's Mary's baby who's God's Son. That's what the angel said. So what's Elizabeth's baby got to do with it?'

'Everything,' says Sarah.

Gruff has stretched himself out beside the fire. John wraps his arms around him and pulls him into his lap.

'Zechariah said these incredible things,' John says. 'He told people that God is going to set them all free – free from all the wrong things they've ever done and will ever do, so they can be close to Him. So they don't ever have to be afraid of Him.'

'So they can be friends with Him,' says Sarah.

John nods. 'And God's going to do that by sending a Saviour. That's the word Zechariah used – Saviour. And the Saviour is Mary's baby – Jesus.'

'Then what about Elizabeth's baby?' asks Benny. 'You still haven't told us what Elizabeth and Zechariah's baby has got to do with it.'

John rolls Gruff over and rubs his furry belly. 'When that little baby grows up – Elizabeth and Zechariah's baby – he's going to tell everyone to get ready for Jesus. He's the one who's going to let people know that, through Jesus, they can be forgiven for everything they've done that's broken their friendship with God – that through Jesus they can be saved.'

Gruff has had enough fuss. He twists over and scrambles out of John's lap. He stands and shakes himself. He watches Saucy as she indulges in an all-over wash, her pale pink tongue working away rhythmically at her paws.

Sarah gazes at her too. 'That's why Jesus will be the Saviour. He'll save people from themselves. He'll save them for God.'

Paul has scratched a 'Z' into the dust. He stares at it. 'Does anyone know how to spell "Zechariah"?'

'Not a clue.' John leans over. He looks at Paul's scribbles. 'But you've missed a name out.'

'Have I? What name?'

John reaches across and takes the stone from his friend. Slowly, making each letter very sharp and very clear, he writes in the dirt beside the fire: 'John'.

Paul frowns. He pushes his glasses up his nose. 'But that's *your* name. Why have you written *your* name?'

'Because that's the name of Zechariah and Elizabeth's baby. That's what the angel told Zechariah to call him: John.'

CHAPTER 8
The Dream
(Matthew 1 v 18–24)

I keep hearing Joseph's secrets.

Sarah sits on the riverbank. There's a spot where it rises just high enough to allow her to dangle her legs over the edge and swirl her feet in the water. It's evening. The sun slips towards the horizon. Streaks and feathers of pink and crimson and orange-red colour the sky. But it's still warm, and Sarah likes the coolness of the river against her skin. Now and again she lifts a foot and watches the streams of water travel down, slip off the ends of her toes and rejoin the running river below.

She talks to God.

I do, God. I keep hearing Joseph's secrets. I don't mean to. I'm not spying. I hope You don't think I'm spying. He just says things and I seem to be there.

I was there when he told someone that he and Mary had got engaged – I knew before everyone else, when it was still a secret! It felt as if I was sharing something with them… as if this special, special thing was happening between Mary and Joseph and their families – and me.

And I was there again today. You know I was there, God. You see everything. I was there when Mary and Joseph got married. I was with Topz. We all saw Mary and she looked so beautiful. I said, 'Joseph must be so proud that she's going to be his wife!' And John said I was being soppy but that's because he didn't want any of us to see that it was making him feel soppy too. It was, though, I know it was.

The sun was blazing down – that sun over there. It's sinking now, so it's not nearly so hot. But then, at the wedding, it was burning. It was burning and I started to feel dizzy. So I went and sat in the shade under the olive trees at the end of the road.

That's when I saw Joseph. I saw Joseph and another man, but they didn't see me. They walked together away from the wedding party. They walked towards me, and stood and talked at the corner of the street.

Joseph said, 'You know I nearly called the wedding off?'

The man with him raised his eyebrows. 'Why?'

'Mary's having a baby,' Joseph said.

The man's eyebrows lifted even further.

'She told me an angel had visited her and given her the news. She told me the baby is God's Son... Well...'

Joseph watched the other man's face. But I watched Joseph.

'How could I marry her?' he said. 'How could I believe her? I mean, what would you have done?'

The man shook his head. He shrugged. What would he have done? 'But you did, Joseph,' he said. 'You have. You just married Mary.'

Joseph looked towards the trees. Towards where I sat in the shadow. He'll see me now, I thought. How can he not see me…?

But he didn't.

'I had a dream,' Joseph said. 'I saw an angel. An angel from God. Perhaps the same angel God sent to Mary, I don't know. But that angel told me not to break our engagement. Not to be afraid to marry Mary.'

Joseph looked back towards the man. He looked him right in the eyes. 'That angel told me Mary's baby is from God. When He's born we're to call Him Jesus. He's going to save people and bring them back to God. His Father God.'

Joseph watched the man. He waited for him to speak. To say something – anything. He looked half worried that his friend wouldn't believe him; half relieved to have been able to tell someone.

The man reached out and placed a hand on Joseph's shoulder. 'Joseph, my friend,' he said, 'what an enormous thing God has asked you and Mary to do.'

I sat so still. I couldn't let them see me now. If they did, they'd know I'd heard everything. Every single word. I held my breath. I tried not to even blink.

'Joseph!' Someone called from further down the road. 'Come on, come back here! No sneaking off on your wedding day!'

The man patted Joseph on the shoulder, then dropped his arm down to his side. 'Thank you, Joseph,' he said. 'Thank you for telling me.'

And then they walked away from me.

Suddenly, it's quite a lot darker. Sarah looks towards the horizon. The sun has gone. Just its glow remains – a pinkish gleam across the lower sky.

She pulls her feet up out of the river. She uses her hands to brush away the water from her skin. Gazing at her washed-clean toes and nails, she draws her knees in to her chest.

I know Joseph's secret, God. I know he almost didn't marry Mary. If he hadn't, she would have had to have her baby all on her own. She would have had to do this whole enormous thing You've asked her to do by herself. With You but no one else. No one on earth to do it with her.

Thank You for sending an angel to Joseph. Thank You for changing his mind. Mary has him beside her now and they can bring up Your Son together.

Mary needs Joseph to be with her, doesn't she? Now more than ever. God, You know us so well. And if You ask us to do something, **YOU NEVER LEAVE US TO STRUGGLE ON OUR OWN.** *Thank You for giving us what we need.*

Thank You for giving Mary and Joseph to each other.

CHAPTER 9
The Long Wait
(Psalm 130 v 6)

It takes a long time to grow a baby – nine months, in fact!

Topz stay close to Nazareth, even when Benny gets the fidgets and wants to move on and explore somewhere else.

'We can go off for a bit,' he says, 'then come back nearer to the time. We don't have to hang around here for the whole of the next few months.'

'Yes, we do,' argues Sarah.

'I think we do too,' says Danny. 'Mary, the baby – they matter too much. I don't want to leave them behind, even for a little while.'

Benny looks put out. 'But it wouldn't be like leaving them behind because we'll be coming back. John? Dave? What about you, Josie? We don't *all* have to be here *all* the time, do we?'

He's wasting his breath. No one wants to go anywhere. This is where Topz want to be. In Nazareth, where Mary and Joseph are.

Benny doesn't sulk for long. Deep inside, he knows

they're right. He has days when he's bored; when he grows tired of the Gang's leapfrog challenges and swimming races at the river; of the games of hopscotch on a grid scratched into the dirt; and of Danny's favourite night-time pursuit – lying down on the ground and counting the stars.

'THERE'S A NEW ONE!' Danny will sometimes shout, and he'll try to point it out – 'There, right there!'

None of them can see it, of course. Mostly, the stars all look the same in their clusters and scatters and the patterns they make. How can they possibly spot a new one in among the millions that are already there? How can even Danny spot one?

No one argues, though, because they want it to be true. They want a new star to be there, and not one member of the Gang wants to be the only one who can't see it.

So, 'Have you spotted it yet?' Danny asks.

And, 'Yes, maybe,' they say. 'Yes, maybe we have.'

Most days, Danny and Sarah in particular make sure they catch a glimpse of Mary. Sometimes she's talking to a neighbour outside her front door, or to Joseph as he works away in his workshop, sawing and hammering and shaping wood. Sometimes she's at the market or carrying washing to the river.

Usually, she looks well and happy. 'Glowing,' says Sarah. 'That's what they say about ladies who are growing babies, isn't it? That they're glowing?'

Other days, Mary seems tired. Tired and a little anxious, especially towards the end of her nine months as the birth gets nearer and nearer.

'I'm sure it's normal,' says Josie, when Sarah worries that something's the matter with Mary or she's not looking after herself properly. 'You must get tired towards the end. You've got all that extra weight to carry around. And it's not as if Mary sits around doing nothing. She's always busy. I know I'd be tired if I were her.'

So the months slip past and the seasons turn, and Mary's baby continues to grow inside her.

Until it's nearly time…

CHAPTER 10

Journey

(Luke 2 v 1–5)

'What's going on?'

Paul and Josie try to push their way through a large knot of people gathered in the street. It seems to grow bigger by the minute. There's a buzz of excited conversation; even the atmosphere seems agitated. The two of them know the rest of the Gang are somewhere up ahead of them – every so often they spot one of them. They just can't reach them through the crowd.

'Sarah!' calls Josie. 'Sarah, wait – what's going on?'

A man turns towards her. 'What's the matter, kid?' he asks. 'What are you yelling for?'

Josie doesn't answer. She doesn't want to. All she cares about is catching up with Topz.

Paul nudges her but she ignores him.

'Erm… sorry.' He turns to the man. 'We're just trying to get to our friends. They're over there somewhere but there are too many people.'

The man tuts. 'You're telling me there are too many people! What a nightmare. Everybody's trying to get to someone – I'm trying to find my brother.'

'Why's everyone out on the street anyway?' Paul asks. 'What's going on?'

'What's going on?' the man repeats. He blinks at Paul. 'Haven't you heard? How can you not have heard?'

The man's response grabs Josie's attention. She gives up with pushing forward and twists round. A couple of steps, jostled by shoulders and elbows, and she stands next to Paul.

'Heard what?' Josie asks.

The man shakes his head. 'Kids these days…' he mutters. **IT'S EMPEROR AUGUSTUS, ISN'T IT? HEARD OF HIM? HE'S ORDERED A CENSUS.'**

'A census?' Paul still looks confused. 'No, sorry, I don't know what you mean.'

'The emperor wants to know how many people there are,' says the man. 'He's ordered everyone to go back to the town where they were born so they can be counted.'

Josie glances at Paul. 'But what about Mary?' she says. 'Mary can't go anywhere.'

'Mary?' The man frowns.

'Mary. She lives here. On that street.' Josie indicates vaguely. 'She's about to have a baby. She could have it any day now, she seriously can't go anywhere.'

'Oh, Mary!' says the man. 'I know who you mean. She's close to her time, isn't she, but – well – an order's an order. She's going to have to go with her husband.'

'But go where?' asks Josie. 'Where was Joseph born?'

The man scratches the side of his nose with a stubby

finger. 'Hmm… now you're asking… I think… I could be wrong, mind, but going by his accent, I think Joseph will have to go to Bethlehem. I've a feeling that's where his family are from.'

Josie looks blank. 'Bethlehem… where's that?'

The man blows out his cheeks in a long sigh. 'It's a fair way from here. I've never been there myself but I'd say it'll take them several days.'

'*What*?' Josie turns to try to peer through the crowd and catch a glimpse of the Gang. She needs to reach them – to tell them!

The man stands, shaking his head. 'Can't say I'd be up for it. It's a brutal journey without being pregnant. But it's not like they've got a choice.'

*　*　*

It is rough for Mary. It's a journey of days, not of hours. There are cold, restless nights and chilly, aching mornings. She has a donkey to carry her but the ride is awkward and uncomfortable. Sometimes she walks beside Joseph to stretch her legs. Sometimes she stops to catch her breath, or to look back towards Nazareth, along the way they've come… then forward towards the miles they still have to cover. And, inside herself, she heaves a sigh.

Topz aren't the only ones who travel the route with them. There are many others. The emperor's census order means people from all over Judea must head to their birthplaces too – to Bethlehem, perhaps, or to Jerusalem, or to other destinations along the way. Whenever Topz stop to look around, they see people on the move.

'I hope Mary gets to Bethlehem in time.' Sarah chews on her bottom lip as she walks. Saucy trots beside her. She began the day tucked into Sarah's leather bag, but she must have got bored. A mile or so back, she'd wriggled out and dropped to the ground.

'You've probably said that at least twenty times since we left Nazareth!' says Benny.

'That's because I'm worried!' replies Sarah. 'I always repeat myself when I'm worried. And I like to think out loud.'

'It'll be all right,' says Danny. 'Mary's not out here on her own.'

'I know that.' Sarah stops gnawing her lip and starts on her thumbnail instead. 'But think what she's going through. It's not ideal, is it, having a baby out here? We're in the middle of nowhere! She's supposed to be at home, where everything is safe and perfect, and Joseph is there to help, and there are lots of people to take care of her. I bet she never imagined in a million years she'd have to drag herself all the way to Bethlehem. Why would she? And what happens if the baby comes before they even get there?'

Josie watches Sarah chewing at her thumb. 'I know it seems hard for Mary,' she says, gently. 'And exhausting and unfair and really, *really* bad timing. But God's with her! We shouldn't forget that. He's in every tiny little detail. God planned it! Don't you think He's got everything under control? He's not going to let anything bad happen to Mary now. Or the baby.'

'Of course He's not.' Danny smiles across at Sarah. **'THIS IS GOD'S BABY. GOD'S ONLY SON.** He's being born for a reason. It's going to be OK.'

Sarah nods slowly. They're right. She knows they're right. But she can't help feeling sad for Mary. She deserves the best possible start for her family.

Josie gives her a nudge. 'I tell you what, though, Sarah,' she says. 'You're going to have to stop chewing your thumb soon or there'll be nothing left.'

'Yeah, just imagine it,' says John. 'And when your thumb's gone, you might start on your hand. And then your arm… Until all that's left of you is your teeth!'

Sarah screws up her face in disgust. 'Trust you to think of something like that.'

'Well, you're the one eating your own thumb!' says John, and he saunters off with a grin.

Danny stands a moment, looking towards the sky. The sun has almost set on another day. The evening chill is closing in. As the shadows deepen, before long the moon will rise and the stars start to appear. Although…

Danny's eyes narrow. There seems to be one star shining already. Growing brighter with the fading light. Brighter and bigger.

It's the biggest star he's ever seen.

CHAPTER 11

Kidnap!

(Micah 5 v 2)

Paul notices first. In the distance, Joseph has stopped walking. Leaning his head towards Mary, he points ahead of him.

Paul scampers closer. Then he throws his arm out in excitement.

'There!' He looks back at the Gang, who start to run towards him. 'Right there!'

And there it is. At first a handful of houses straggle along the road. Then more and more. Still a little way off yet, but clearly a small town.

The town of Bethlehem.

'MARY MADE IT!' A grin spreads across Sarah's face.

They speed up, no longer dragging their feet. There's a fresh energy to their steps.

Joseph picks up his pace, too. He leads the donkey, with Mary settled on its back, more purposefully; more positively. They've followed orders and travelled for miles, and at long last their goal is in sight. Before much longer, they'll be walking the streets of Bethlehem.

Gruff senses the excitement and starts to dash in circles.

He runs away from John, twists round and pelts back to him, making the rest of the Gang laugh.

'Crazy dog!' John laughs the most. 'Crazy, mad dog!'

Sarah lifts Saucy and slips her back into her bag. 'You're crazy mad too,' she whispers in her ear, 'and I don't want you running off.'

As they pass the first houses, there are more and more people. Some are travellers, dust from the road clinging to their clothes. Others live in Bethlehem, and have come out to watch the hordes arriving in their town.

There are men in uniform too – just a few here and there. Sarah watches them. She doesn't know why, but they make her feel uncomfortable.

'Who do you suppose they are?' she asks.

Danny shrugs. 'They look like soldiers.' With his eyes he follows a perfectly straight, firm-footed, uniformed man who strides past. 'There's a lot of people here. Maybe they have to keep an eye on things.'

'Maybe…' says Sarah, but she still doesn't like it. The uncomfortable feeling doesn't go away.

Someone giggles. Danny turns his head.

A girl stands with her back against a low, square building. She looks about his age, perhaps a little older. She watches Gruff as he dashes around in circles, bounds away, then returns to John.

Danny catches her eye. 'His name's Gruff.'

'Mad crazy Gruff,' says John. 'You need to calm down, boy, or I'll have to carry you. There are too many people here.'

The girl says nothing, but the smile on her lips stays as she watches Gruff's antics.

Topz move on, the crowds around them growing thicker. There are horses, too, tied at the side of the street. A soldier stands next to one of them and adjusts its bridle.

'We're going to lose Mary and Joseph in amongst all these people,' says Sarah. 'If that happens we won't know where they're staying. It'll take ages to find them again!'

'It won't take ages.' Benny shakes his head. 'Bethlehem can't be that big. And there can't be that many people about to have a baby. Someone will know where they are.'

Another soldier brushes past. His long cloak ripples as he walks.

Up ahead, Joseph and Mary turn down a narrow road. Topz hurry to keep up. It's a struggle against the tide of people surging towards them.

'There's no room anywhere.' A woman's voice. She holds a small boy by the hand. 'We're not going to find anywhere to stay.'

John turns to look at them.

'There'll be somewhere,' mutters the man next to her. 'Let's keep looking. Come here, you.'

He turns to the boy, picks him up and hoists him onto his shoulders.

The woman shakes her head. 'I wish we'd got here a couple of days ago. This is hopeless.'

'Did you hear that?' John touches Danny on the shoulder. 'There's nowhere to stay. People are saying that everywhere is full.'

Danny nods his head towards Joseph. 'There'll be somewhere for Mary. Joseph seems to know where he's going.'

As John glances down to look for Gruff, that's when he realises he can't see him – anywhere.

Then, suddenly, there's a shout: 'Wait! Stop! Wait!'

A girl shoves her way towards them. She pushes into people; stumbles past people. It's the smiling girl they'd seen at the entrance to Bethlehem – but she's not smiling anymore.

'A soldier took your dog…' she gasps, breathlessly, as she finally reaches them. She stares into their faces. They don't say a word.

'Did you hear what I said?' The girl jabs an arm out behind her. *'A soldier just took your dog!'*

John's mouth falls open. 'No!' He looks all around him. 'Gruff! *Gruff*!' His gaze flicks between people's trampling feet. He turns a full circle. 'Gruff? Gruff!' The panic sets in to his voice and his eyes.

'He's gone!' the girl yells. 'A soldier just took him! He rode off with him on a horse.'

John goes to run in the direction she's pointing.

Danny grabs hold of him.

'Woah, wait a second!' He turns back to the girl. 'What soldier? Do you know where he's going?'

The girl rests her hands on her hips, still breathing heavily. 'He's one of those from King Herod's court. There's been loads of them here over the last few days. All to do with this census.'

'King Herod's court...' John looks as though he might

burst into tears. 'Where's that?'

The girl raises her eyebrows. 'You really are from out of town, aren't you? It's in Jerusalem.'

'Jerusalem…' John's mind races. 'Then I've got to go after him. How far is it?'

'Not that far. A few miles, maybe.'

John makes to move again but Danny keeps hold of him. 'You're sure it was Gruff?' he says to the girl. 'You're totally sure?'

'Of course I'm sure. A crazy, mad, little brown dog. He was still being crazy and mad when the soldier grabbed him.'

At last John manages to shake Danny off. 'I'm going to Jerusalem!' he yells over his shoulder. All thoughts of Mary and Joseph have been blasted away. 'I'll meet you back here when I've found my dog.'

Danny glances after him, then back towards the girl. 'Can you find our friends? The ones we were with before? They're up there somewhere. I think they've turned off.' He jerks his head towards the narrow road.

The girl shrugs. 'I can try.'

'Please tell them where we're going – tell them we'll meet them back here in Bethlehem.' He starts to run. 'Find them and tell them we'll be back!'

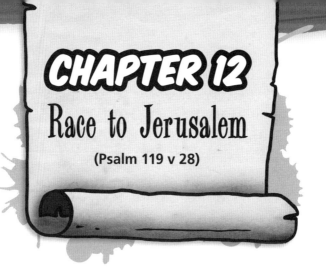

CHAPTER 12
Race to Jerusalem
(Psalm 119 v 28)

'John! John, wait!' Danny runs after him as fast as he can, past the last few houses and out onto the open road. 'John, wait, I'm coming with you!'

John glances over his shoulder. He slows but he doesn't stop.

Danny catches up with him and sees the tears on his friend's face.

'I should have been watching him,' John stammers. 'Gruff. I should have had my eye on him or I should have carried him. This should never have happened. It's all my fault!'

'It's not your fault.' Danny falls in step with him. 'How could you have known someone was going to snatch him? It's not you who's done anything wrong, it's that soldier!'

'But why did he take him?' More tears fall. 'Why would anybody take someone else's dog?'

'I don't know.' Danny shakes his head. 'But we'll find him, John. We'll get him back.'

'But what if we don't? I'll never see him again!

I'll never know what's happened to him!'

'We'll find him.' Danny sounds more confident than he feels. What else can he say? 'We'll ask God and – we'll find him.'

Once again, they're not alone on the road. Just as on the route to Bethlehem, there are others making their way to Jerusalem. Now and again soldiers pass on horseback.

'I wish we had a horse,' John mumbles. 'We'd get there quicker.'

'We'll get there soon,' Danny says. 'That girl said it's not very far.'

A short distance ahead, a man is leading a donkey. There's a woven rug on its back and several baskets are roped together and slung across its shoulders. The donkey's ears are pricked and alert as it picks its way along the road. John and Danny jog up behind it, and the ears swivel towards them at the sound of their footsteps.

The man turns. For a second he looks alarmed, as if he expects to be attacked and robbed! But when he sees the runners are young boys, he relaxes.

'Sorry,' says John. 'Didn't mean to make you jump. Are we nearly in Jerusalem?'

The man points. 'Just over the hill. You'll see it soon enough.'

John breaks into a run and Danny chases after him.

'What's the hurry?' calls the man, but they don't hear him.

At the brow of the hill they stop. They gasp for breath. Danny's legs quiver like jelly under his body.

He's exhausted. He knows John's worn out too, but there's no point saying it. There's no point even thinking it. They just need to push on.

After Nazareth and Bethlehem, Jerusalem seems very grand. Bigger; more imposing. Wealthier. It's busy here too.

John stops and looks around, scanning the cityscape for a soldier; for a small brown dog…

He throws up his hands. 'Now what, Danny? Now what do we do? Gruff could be anywhere! This place is huge! I don't even know where to *start* looking.'

Danny desperately wracks his brain. If only Paul were there. Paul's usually the genius – the one with all the ideas. If Paul were there, what would he say? What would he do?

Suddenly, Danny jerks his head up. 'The king's in charge, right?'

John nods. 'Yes, I suppose. King Herod.'

Danny's face brightens with a grin. 'Then, wouldn't he like to know that one of his soldiers is a thief?'

John looks blank.

'Oh, come on, John, keep up!' There's excitement in Danny's voice now. 'We'll tell King Herod that one of his soldiers stole Gruff, and he'll get him back for us.'

John takes this in slowly. 'So, we just march into the palace for a chat with the king? Do you honestly think that will work?'

'We'll figure it out when we get there.' Danny starts to march confidently along the street, with John running after him. 'Anyway,' he adds, 'have you got a better idea?'

CHAPTER 13

Lydia*

(Luke 2 v 7)

Sarah hugs Saucy close and tight.

'I can't believe it,' she sobs. 'I can't believe Gruff's gone!' She nuzzles a damp cheek into Saucy's fur.

The girl watches her. 'Sorry. I had to tell you. The other boy asked me to.'

'And you're sure they've gone to Jerusalem?' asks Dave. 'They've left already?'

The girl nods.

'We should go after them,' Benny says. 'We should help them find Gruff.'

'I think we should probably stay here,' says Dave, stroking Saucy's head. 'Danny said to stay here.'

'I think you're right,' says Paul. 'At least Danny and John know where we are. If we go to Jerusalem too, we'll lose each other.'

'And we've come all this way because of Mary,' says Josie. 'They'd want us to stay close to her and make sure everything's all right with the baby.'

Sarah turns back to the girl. 'Are you here for the census?'

'No, I live here.' The girl jerks a thumb over her shoulder. 'That's my house back there – where I saw you when you first got here.'

'What's your name?'

'Lydia.'

'Hello, Lydia.' Sarah tries to smile. 'I'm Sarah. Gruff belongs to John. John's my brother.'

Josie looks up and down the road. She scans all the different faces; the visitors and the locals; the people in a hurry; the people who seem to have all the time in the world. But there's no sign of the ones she's looking for.

'Erm… Sorry to bring this up but – does anyone know which way Mary and Joseph went?'

*   *   *

Lydia knows every inch of Bethlehem. She knows who lives on which street and how many there are in each family. She knows who owns a donkey and who runs a market stall. She knows the main streets and the back streets – all the shortcuts.

And she knows of every inn and guesthouse in the town.

Topz traipse with her from one to another, to another. When Lydia asks the innkeepers whether they've seen Mary and Joseph, the answer's always the same: 'Of course I remember them – that poor woman looked as if she was about to give birth. But we're fully booked and bursting at the seams. I had to send them away to try somewhere else.'

Dejected, Benny kicks at the ground. His face is sullen. His empty stomach growls.

'I can't believe we've come all this way and now we've lost them,' he grumbles. 'We've lost them *and* Gruff. Brilliant.'

'THERE IS ONE MORE PLACE,' says Lydia. 'It's on the other side of town. It's probably full too, but the innkeeper there is nice. He's always really helpful. It's worth a try.'

They walk on. Sarah still carries Saucy in her arms – she doesn't want to put her back in her bag. At least with her arms wrapped around her, she knows her precious cat is safe. Not like Gruff. Poor Gruff. Poor John…

Before they even reach the inn, it's obvious all the rooms are taken. As they near the building, they see the gathering of travellers hovering outside. There's no point, of course. The visitors might wait for the rest of the day but the chances of a room suddenly becoming free are virtually non-existent. But they hang around in hope anyway.

'We can ask at least,' says Lydia. 'Maybe Mary and Joseph got the last room.'

Mary and Joseph hadn't got the last room. By the time they'd arrived, there wasn't so much as a broom cupboard going spare. The same as all across Bethlehem.

But Mary was exhausted, worn out and on the edge of tears, and Joseph was desperate. And the innkeeper couldn't turn his back on them. Supposing Mary had been his daughter? A long way from home, about to give birth and with nowhere to stay? No.

This innkeeper wasn't having that.

The man eyes the group of children in front of him. 'Why are you asking, Lydia? You don't know them, do you? Not all the way from Nazareth?'

'No, but…' Lydia glances at Topz. 'My friends here do. They've come from Nazareth too.'

'Well, we don't *know them* exactly,' Josie quickly adds, 'but we know Mary's having a baby, and she and Joseph have had to come such a long way at a really difficult time. We just want to make sure she's all right. You know – safe.'

'Oh, they're safe enough,' says the innkeeper. **I'VE GOT A STABLE ROUND THE BACK.** I told them they can stay there. I mean, the animals are in there,' he admits, 'but there's water and I've put in some clean straw. And it'll be warmer for them than out here in the street. I know it's not the most comfortable place to have a baby, but I'm afraid it's the best I can do.'

'Definitely better than nothing,' Dave beams. 'Sounds great – thank you!'

Lydia smiles at her innkeeper friend. 'I was sure you'd help if you could.' She glances at Topz. 'Do you want to go and say hello?'

'Actually, I suggest you leave them be for now,' says the innkeeper, shaking his head. 'What that young lady needs now is privacy. Peace and quiet and privacy. Now, go on, off you hop. I can't stand around here talking all afternoon. I've got an inn full of guests to look after. Pop back in the morning, if you want to, and I'll let you know how she is.'

Pop back in the morning…?

Topz look at each other. Morning is a long way off. They've nowhere to stay themselves. They've had nothing to eat. They're not even sure where they might be able to set up camp.

And then there's the fact that Gruff is still missing!

'Do you like sheep?' Lydia stands in front of them, her arms folded, her chin tilted towards them.

'Sheep?' repeats Sarah.

'Yes, sheep,' says Lydia. 'My father's a shepherd. He has lots of them.'

'Oh,' Sarah says, still not sure this is relevant.

'I've got one too. Would you like to meet her?'

'Well… yes, all right.'

It's not as if they have anything better to do!

'Come on, then, let's go,' says Lydia. 'We can get something to eat too. When my father camps out, he always has a big pot of stew.'

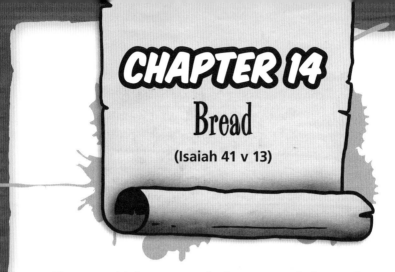

CHAPTER 14

Bread

(Isaiah 41 v 13)

Danny and John gaze at the huge gates in front of them. They rise up, tall and commanding.

The Topz boys know they've done the easy bit. They've found the palace. Now, not only do they have to find a way in… they have to find a way to reach the king.

'Supposing we just walk in,' says John. 'Maybe we could say our parents work here. We could say that, couldn't we?'

'Maybe we could just *ask* to see the king,' says Danny.

John sighs. 'No one's *ever* going to let us see the king. You know they're not.'

John's right, but what choice do they have? If they try to sneak in and then they get caught, how does that help Gruff? King Herod will think *they* are thieves, and will never believe they're here to rescue a dog!

A young woman bustles towards them. She carries a deep basket full of small loaves of bread. She seems in a hurry. She's focused on where she's going and hardly notices the boys. They step back out of her way.

Whether she trips on the lumpy ground or, in her

rush, her long cloak gets caught around her ankles, the boys don't know. But as she loses her balance, she might still have been able to right herself... if it wasn't for John.

John does try to help by reaching out to save the basket. But it's a wrong move. There's a collision; a tangle of arms and scuffling feet. One minute the woman is on her way to the palace kitchen with supplies, the next she's sprawled on the ground, John in a heap beside her. The basket is on its side and almost all the bread rolls are scattered in the dust.

She scrambles up quickly, and her grazed hands fly to her mouth.

'OH NO! WHAT HAVE I DONE?' She looks at John, who still sits on the ground. 'What have you made me do?'

Her eyes dart about furtively. Has anyone noticed? If they have, she'll be in trouble – such trouble! She's already late and now this!

There are soldiers on duty by the main entrance to the palace. If they've seen, they don't appear to care. Some woman has fallen over and dropped her delivery. It makes no difference to them.

John gets to his feet and stands up the basket. Danny squats down to gather up the rolls.

'You don't have to do that. Leave them!' snaps the woman.

She starts to pick them up herself. Some of the crusts look battered. Others are flecked with dirt.

'What am I going to do?' she says in a raised, angry voice, but then checks herself – noise will only attract attention. Lowering her tone to a rasping whisper, she demands, 'How can I deliver these to the king now?'

'They're not so bad,' says Danny. 'Look, it all brushes off. It's just a bit of dust.'

'Just a bit of dust?' The woman looks at Danny as if he were from another planet. 'These are for the *king*!'

'I'm really sorry…' John inspects the palms of his hands. They're sore, and he tries to rub the dirt away on his tunic. 'I honestly didn't mean to. I was trying to help.'

'Help?' the woman splutters. 'By getting under my feet? Very helpful indeed!'

She picks up the last of the bread and straightens up, and it's in that moment that John and Danny are both struck by the same idea.

'Well – we could come in with you.' Danny gives John a sideways look.

'That's right,' John says. 'We could say it wasn't your fault. I got in your way and tripped you up. After all, it's what I did.'

The woman stares at them. 'Why would you want to do that? Why would anyone do that? Why should you care if I get in trouble or not?'

John shrugs. 'I just feel bad.'

The woman hesitates. As it stands, either way she's in trouble – whether she delivers a basketful of dirty bread to the palace kitchen, or she doesn't deliver it and her older sister, who baked it, gives her a serious piece of her mind.

At least if these boys go with her they can take a share of the blame.

'Fine, then.' The woman gives a brief nod. 'And for being so clumsy,' – she narrows her eyes at John – 'you can carry the basket.'

John picks it up. The woman is already stomping off ahead of them. There's no time to think or decide if this is really the best plan – they just need to follow.

The woman doesn't make for the main entrance. Instead, she cuts diagonally across the wide courtyard and heads down the side of the building. The boys scurry along after her.

They quickly arrive at a low door in the palace wall, out of sight of the main gates. The woman opens it.

'Come on, keep up,' she urges, and steps inside the palace.

John and Danny slip through behind her.

It takes a moment for their eyes to adjust. Walking in from bright daylight, at first the dimness seems almost pitch black. It's cold, too – not at all how you might imagine a palace – but this is probably a back entrance, and not one King Herod ever uses.

The boys find themselves in a narrow corridor. The woman is already marching along it. They can hear her more clearly than they can see her. She stops at a patch of light that falls into the passageway from the right.

The light escapes through a tall arched opening.

'In here,' the woman says.

The three of them step through to the palace kitchen.

'You're late!' A voice, sharp and irritated, squawks at them the moment they appear in the room. The man it belongs to looks as angry as his voice. His eyes flick towards John and Danny almost at once.

'I'm sorry, I'm sorry,' says the woman. 'I was running a bit behind and then this little pest...' – she bats John on the shoulder with the back of her hand – 'knocks me flying.'

The man eyes the two boys.

'I just wanted to say I'm sorry,' mumbles John. 'It was my fault, so please don't shout at her. And I'm sorry about the bread too.'

Instantly, the man's eyes drop to the contents of the basket. They widen slightly as he takes in the dirty and slightly battered rolls.

'And what am I supposed to do with these?' he asks indignantly.

'We'll clean them up for you, if you like,' says Danny. 'It won't take long.'

'Won't it?' The man nods sarcastically. 'Won't it indeed?' He steps forward and shoves his face close to Danny's. 'You do realise these are for the king's supper table, don't you? I'm not sure a bit of cleaned up bread roll is going to be good enough for King Herod!'

'I did tell him that,' the woman interrupts.

'In fact,' continues the angry man, 'this bread doesn't even look fit for that mangy dog out there!'

Mangy *dog*?

John and Danny look at each other.

What dog? It can't be Gruff. No one could ever describe Gruff as *mangy*. He was scruffy, yes. And since he liked to roll in the dust to scratch himself all over if ever he had an itch, it was a struggle to keep him clean. But no one could call him mangy. Except perhaps for an angry man who likes giving orders and is in charge of the king's food.

IT CAN'T BE GRUFF... CAN IT?

The man takes the basket from John and drops it on a large table. 'Now,' he says, turning back to them, 'you stay here until that bread's fit for a king. Every last crumb. Understand?'

The boys nod.

The woman shuffles towards the door. 'I've got to go. Lots more deliveries to make. Like I say, that boy made the mess, not me. It's up to him to sort it out.'

And she's gone.

The man doesn't attempt to stop her. As John and Danny start to pick at the loaves, he stands over them. He watches every move they make.

'So,' says John, 'what's with the dog?'

The man doesn't take his eagle eyes from the boys' busy fingers. 'What's it to you?'

'Oh, nothing,' says John. 'I just like dogs, that's all.'

'Really?' The man couldn't sound less interested. 'Well, this one's not very likeable. I've never seen a dog with such a miserable expression. Some solider brought it here earlier.'

John's heart seems to leap into his throat. 'Earlier? Where from?'

The man scowls at him. 'How am I supposed to know?'

'Just wondering,' John mumbles, trying to hide the emotion in his voice. 'Not sure why someone would bring a scruffy old dog to a palace.' He tries to clean up the bread between his fingers but he's too distracted to look at it properly.

'Tch!' The man shakes his head impatiently. 'I think he

thought he could sell it to the king. Something to keep His Majesty entertained. "You should see it," he says, "it dashes about like a mad thing."'

John's fingers freeze. A mad thing? It has to be Gruff!

'Sounds like a fun dog...' Danny says quietly.

'Not really!' scoffs the man. 'It just mopes. And when it's not moping, it's whining. What's the king going to want with a dog that mopes and whines? He's hardly going to pay good money for that, is he? So now we're stuck with it. The soldier left it out in the kitchen yard to settle in, but it'll never settle in and the king will never want it. No, if it doesn't cheer up by tomorrow, I'll have to get rid of it.'

Hands on hips, the man leans over the two boys, so close they can feel his warm breath on their faces.

'Now,' he says, 'enough of the chit-chat. Just hurry up and finish what you're doing so you can get out from under my feet.'

CHAPTER 15
Shepherds in the Hills
(Luke 2 v 8)

Lydia stands at the top of the hill and points.

The valley below is speckled with the grey-white blobs of fluffy sheep. They graze peacefully. A few lie on the short grass, legs tucked up beneath them, dozing.

As Topz gaze down, a fire draws their eyes. It's only the afternoon and there's still a vague warmth to the sun, but a group of shepherds already huddle around it. Most importantly, one of them stirs the large pot that sits over the flames.

'That'll be the stew, won't it?' says Benny. He's starving. His mouth waters at the word.

Lydia nods. 'Come on,' she says. She starts to scramble down the hillside. 'Come and meet my dad. Then you can say hello to my sheep!'

Lydia often heads out to spend time with her father when he's shepherding the flock in the hills around Bethlehem. She likes to pretend she's a shepherd too. She knows exactly what to do – how to herd the animals together, how to count them and keep track of them. She could probably even put up some sort of defence if a wild animal tried to attack them – especially if the attack was aimed at her own little sheep! She'd had it since it was a tiny lamb. Nothing was going to happen to that little creature, not on her watch.

'Are there really attacks?' Sarah asks.

'Sometimes,' says Lydia. 'Wolves, mostly.' She doesn't sound at all concerned.

Sarah, on the other hand, starts to cast a wary eye around her. She pulls the bag with Saucy inside closer to her.

'Wolves!' exclaims Benny. 'That's fantastic! I'd love to see a wolf!'

'Have you seen one?' Paul asks.

'I've seen several,' Lydia replies. 'I've seen my dad chase them away.' She says it as if it's nothing. Just something to be expected if you're a shepherd – which it probably is.

Before they reach the shepherds at the campfire, they hear bleating.

Lydia stops. She turns her head and smiles. She walks towards the dumpy-looking sheep that trots in her direction. She crouches down and takes its face in her hands.

'Hello,' she says. 'I've brought visitors to see you.'

The sheep tosses its head slightly, as if it really doesn't care less. Lydia is here, fussing her head, her ears. Lydia's visit is all that matters.

'Her name's Deborah,' Lydia says.

Topz don't move. They know sheep can be timid.

'It's all right,' Lydia says. 'You can come over and stroke her.'

The Gang step towards Deborah. The sheep eyes them suspiciously at first. But Lydia is calm and unworried. And as the hands reach out to stroke the bony head, the woolly back, Deborah almost looks pleased about the attention.

'I've never touched a sheep before,' Sarah whispers.

'Neither have I,' says Dave. 'I don't think any of us have.'

'Really?' Lydia raises her eyebrows – imagine never having touched a sheep. 'Nothing feels quite like sheep's wool,' she says. 'It's thick and oily and I love the smell.'

Lydia's father watches her make her way towards him, Deborah at her heels and Topz following on behind.

'I've brought friends,' Lydia says.

'So I see,' says her father. 'Friends from where?'

'Nazareth. They've come to Bethlehem for the census. At least, they've come to Bethlehem because someone they know who's come to Bethlehem for the census is having a baby.'

'Is that so?' says her father. Like Lydia, his voice is very calm. Very steady.

'And… Dad?'

He leans forward and gives the stew another stir. 'Yes, Lydia?'

'They're very hungry.'

CHAPTER 16

Escape

(Psalm 120 v 1)

John drops the last bread roll back into the basket.

'Sand,' he growls. 'We're wasting our time flicking sand off bread rolls when what we should be doing is rescuing Gruff!'

'We will…' Danny glances over his shoulder at the angry man. 'Just hang on.'

The man in charge of the kitchen has finally moved away to inspect some water jars lined up against the far wall. He straightens up. Danny sees the dissatisfied glare in his eye.

'Why are these water jars empty?' The man barks across to some women who are preparing fruit. 'Full, I said. They all need to be full. One of you, stop what you're doing and go to the well.'

But none of the women move. One just gives a brief nod of her head.

The man is distracted and Danny seizes the opportunity. 'We've finished,' he calls out.

Dismissively, the man waves him away. He doesn't take his eyes off the women and his face clouds over.

'So, come on,' he says. 'Who's going to get the water?'

'I'll go,' says the woman who nodded before. 'I'll just finish this first.'

'No!' snaps the man. 'Let them finish that. You fill these jars.'

Danny starts to push John towards the door.

The man doesn't notice. He's too flustered by the lack of water.

'Why do I have to say these things over and over again?' the man complains as he watches the woman wipe off her hands. 'If it wasn't for me, the king would probably never eat or drink at all!'

He's still ranting as John and Danny dive through the archway.

'Where now?' John twists his head one way, then the other.

'Not that way, that's the way we came in.' Danny points behind him. 'It leads straight back out of the palace.'

There's a yell behind them.

'GET BACK HERE!'

Eyes popping, Danny turns John round and shoves him. 'That way!' he hisses.

They run for it down the corridor away from the kitchen. They can't see much in the dimness. They hold their arms out in front of them to save themselves in case they bump in to anything. Or anyone…

It seems there's only one way to go. The passage turns sharply to the right. They follow it round.

Out of sight of the kitchen doorway, they hesitate. What now?

They can hear the man's shouts. He's still cross about the empty water jars, but he yells for the boys to come back too. Will he come after them?

John turns, starting to panic. A short way ahead of them is a door. It's solid apart from a small metal grill cut into the top half. Through the narrow bars seeps daylight.

There are no other doors. No other turnings.

John looks back at Danny. 'It's the only way out.'

Danny shrugs his shoulders. 'Then that's the way we've got to go!'

John grabs hold of the thick iron loop that lifts the latch on the door and gives it a twist. It's stiff and awkward. It takes him three tries to get it to budge.

Then there's a clunk and the harsh scrape of metal against metal as the latch shifts, and the door opens.

Their eyes are pierced instantly by the broad daylight. They squint into it, blinking as they adjust from the darkness of the corridor.

They see bare walls in front of them, a lot taller than they are, enclosing a sandy yard. There are stacks of baskets. Stone water jars stand in lines, upright like soldiers, and a few bulging sacks are slumped in a corner like sleepy old men.

There are other bits and pieces too, but that's all they have time to take in before it hits them.

Something small and wild catapults itself towards them from the ground. John staggers back with the force of it. There are buffeting paws and a licking tongue and a high-pitched yelping that could only

ever mean one thing: they've found each other!
Inadvertently, they've stumbled on the kitchen yard.
GRUFF AND JOHN ARE BACK TOGETHER!

A moment later, Gruff leaps on Danny. He wriggles and kicks and licks him all over his face.

John grapples with the little dog. He tries to calm him enough so that at least he's quiet. But it's almost impossible. The excitement and the relief are too much – for both of them.

Danny moves towards a barred gate in the facing wall. It's tall – much taller than he is. As high as the walls.

Danny peers through. He can see that the gate will lead them out of the palace, but they'll still be within the royal courtyard. That means having to leave through the entrance gates in full view of the soldiers. And how far will they get?

He places his hand on the latch and lifts. Nothing happens. The gate doesn't budge.

He does the same thing again, but this time with a shove.

Again, nothing.

'I think it's locked!' he hisses towards John.

'No!' John looks crushed. 'That means we'll have to go back past the kitchen. What if we don't make it?'

A figure appears in the doorway. John has his back to it, so at first he doesn't see. What he does see is the expression of horror that creeps across his friend's face.

CHAPTER 17
A Jealous King
(Matthew 2 v 1–8)

The woman who stands in the doorway holds a water jar up on her shoulder. She looks at Danny, then towards John.

Gruff is still an excited, wriggling bundle in John's arms. His stubby tail wags so fast it's just a blur.

The woman – the one from the kitchen who's been ordered to fetch water – doesn't look worried, or angry, or as if she's about to call for help.

She just looks puzzled.

'He's his dog, you see,' Danny says quietly. 'He's John's dog. Gruff's his name. Gruff. And the soldier who brought him here for the king stole him. So we've come to take him back.'

The woman still says nothing.

'He stopped being all crazy and fun because he wasn't with John and he was sad. But I promise you,' Danny finishes, 'we're not doing anything wrong. Gruff really is John's dog.'

It's obvious. Dogs greet long-lost friends like… long-lost friends. Gruff and John love each other. It's plain to see.

Still with the jar held on her shoulder, the woman walks towards the gate. She produces a large, heavy-looking key, shoves it into the lock and turns it. It's creaky and stiff, but it gives. She lifts the latch and the gate swings open.

Danny watches the woman's face. What's she thinking? Will she call the soldier? Will they be arrested?

She gives a faint smile and jerks her head towards the opening. She stands aside to let the boys through.

'Walk with me,' she says. 'I'll go to the well outside the gates. We'll walk there together. No one will stop you if you're with me.'

Danny makes a face. 'They might if they see us with this dog…'

The woman gazes at him a moment, then glances round.

'There,' she says, nodding towards a stack of crates against the wall. 'Use a basket.'

Danny's eyes light up. Perfect! He grabs a smallish one and they slip Gruff inside.

'You've got to stay quiet now, Gruff,' pleads John. 'Quiet and still.'

Danny digs around among the sacks and finds a couple of empty ones. He folds one of them and covers Gruff, tucking it in around him.

With John holding the basket, they walk down the alley beside the palace and out into the wide, open courtyard. In full view of the soldiers on duty at the main entrance, they make for the gate.

Please, God… The same prayer runs through both

boys' heads. *Please, God, help us get out…*

There's a sudden shout from behind them: **'HEY!'**

It's a solider. The three of them stop in their tracks. Calmly, the woman with the jar turns.

'If you're going to the well, bring us some water back, will you?' calls the soldier.

The woman smiles and nods, then turns back and carries on walking. The boys keep just slightly behind.

Once through the gates she says, 'On your way. Keep the basket. Your dog will be safer in there. Keep him out of sight till you're away.'

'Thanks. Thank you.' It doesn't seem enough, but John doesn't know what else to say.

Danny says nothing. He's distracted. There are three smartly-dressed men in the palace courtyard. He stops to look at them.

They must be wealthy. Their clothes look fancy and expensive. They have camels with them with lots of baggage slung across the coarse hair on their backs.

'Maybe they're the reason the kitchen manager's in such a panic,' Danny says. 'Important guests for dinner with the king, do you think?'

'I don't think they're eating with the king.' The woman watches them. 'Not this one anyway. **KING HEROD ISN'T THE KING THEY'RE LOOKING FOR.'**

Danny raises an eyebrow. 'Do you mean there's another one?'

Still holding Gruff in the basket, John fidgets from foot to foot. Gruff wriggles under the sack cover. He's impatient too.

'Danny, we need to get out of here,' John says.

'He's right, you should go,' says the woman.

Danny is still curious. 'We will, but – who's the other king?'

'No idea. I only know King Herod isn't happy about it.'

'Why not?'

The woman shakes her head. 'I was collecting dirty goblets from the wine steward. I didn't hear them myself, but the steward told me those men had been asking King Herod about a new king. A king who was just a baby – who might not even have been born yet. They said they were astronomers or something. They spent their time studying the skies and they'd noticed a new star. It was very big and very bright. It just appeared out of nowhere. They said that's how they knew a brand-new king was about to be born – that's what the star meant.'

Danny's eyes go wide. *He's* seen a star, just a few nights ago on the journey from Nazareth to Bethlehem. One he's sure he's never noticed before; bigger and brighter than all the others.

John's eye stretch wide too. A king? A king who hasn't been born yet? Didn't the angel tell Mary her baby would be a king?

'Anyway,' the woman says, 'the steward said the men told King Herod they'd followed the star for miles to find this new king. They'd come all this way to bring him gifts and to worship him.'

John takes a few steps closer to peer back through the gate. He watches the three men with their camels.

'I saw that star,' says Danny. 'I'm sure I saw it.'

'Well,' says the woman, 'King Herod apparently said he couldn't help them. He didn't know anything about a new king. But he told the men to wait and he'd see whether some of the priests in Jerusalem might have an idea.'

'And did they?' asks Danny.

'Yes. Unfortunately, they did. Well – unfortunately for the baby.'

John frowns. 'Why?'

The woman looks at him curiously. **'DON'T YOU KNOW ANYTHING ABOUT KING HEROD?'**

The boys gaze back with blank expressions.

'He's not a kind man,' she says, 'not at all. And he's very jealous. The steward said the priests told the king that God had made a promise a long, long time ago. A prophet had written about it: the new king would be born in Bethlehem.'

John catches his breath. He's right. The new king the men are looking for is Mary's baby. The Saviour of the world! The star they've been following is for Jesus!

'And?' The frown on Danny's face deepens.

The woman says, 'King Herod told the three men that, after they've been to Bethlehem and found the baby king, they're to come back here to Jerusalem and let him know exactly where he is – so that he can go and worship him too. Which is about when I turned up to collect the goblets. I saw the men leave. I heard what King Herod said after they'd gone.'

'What? What did he say?'

'He said he hoped they'd come back quickly. Because as soon as he knew where the baby was, he wasn't going to worship him. He was going to kill him.'

CHAPTER 18
Angels in the Sky
(Luke 2 v 9–15)

The light is fading fast. The hills stand still and silent, dark against an even darker sky.

Benny shivers and huddles closer to the fire. Topz sit with Lydia around the flames. The yellow-orange glow sends shadows dancing on their faces. Their breath shows in misty clouds in the cold evening air.

'We should go soon,' says Sarah. She gazes down at Saucy, curled in her lap. She watches her cat's slow breathing; enjoys her warmth against her. 'When John and Danny get back to Bethlehem, they won't know where we are.'

Dave throws another chunk of wood onto the burning pile. The shepherds have gone off on patrol, checking on the scattered sheep and keeping a wary eye out for predators now that night is falling. Before they left, they told their guests to keep the fire bright.

'They may not come back tonight,' Dave says. 'John won't leave Gruff behind, I know he won't. He won't leave Jerusalem till they've found him.'

Sarah wants to cry again. Perhaps more tears would

make her feel better. Only, they won't come. She feels empty inside. But at the same time, she knows that something wonderful is about to happen. Something that will change the world forever. Mary will be a new mother soon and God's Son will be alive on the earth.

If only it felt real. She just wants it to feel real…

Sarah senses Josie's arm around her shoulders. She looks round but her friend suddenly pulls it away and scrambles to her feet.

Josie stares into the sky. Sarah glances up to follow her gaze.

'LOOK AT THAT STAR!'

'That can't be a star,' murmurs Paul. 'It's too big. Isn't it? I've never seen a star like that before.'

'Nor have I,' says Benny. 'But that's a star all right! Biggest star in the whole universe, but definitely a star.'

'I wish Danny was here.' Josie blinks in its brightness. 'He'd love it.'

'If it looks this big from here,' says Lydia, 'he can probably see it from Jerusalem.'

She turns and peers through the dimness to try to catch sight of her father and the shepherds with him. They must have noticed it too.

She steps away from the fire. She can just about make out their shapes a little way off. She starts to walk towards them.

Then she stops.

The shepherds all stare up into the sky too, but they're not looking at the star. They're gazing away from it.

Lydia turns. Instantly she sees what they see. She sucks in enough breath to call: 'Sarah!'

High above them is what looks like a ball of fire. It seems to be falling out of the sky. It grows bigger. And bigger. Much bigger than the star.

As Topz reach Lydia, from somewhere behind her, her father shouts, 'Lydia! Run!'

But she can't run. None of them can run. Not even the shepherds. They're frozen to the spot. Instinctively, even Saucy has dived for cover within the safety of Sarah's bag.

The fireball drops down and down – closer and closer. Until it slows. Until it stops right over the heads of the shepherds!

They crouch down. They daren't look any longer. They lift their arms to protect themselves.

It's Sarah who understands first. She understands because she's seen this once before.

This isn't a ball of fire. This blaze – this intense, brilliant blaze – is an angel.

'Look up!' The angel speaks, smiling down at the terrified shepherds. 'Don't be frightened. Look up and see! I've come from God. He's sent me here to bring you good news. Good news that will bring comfort and joy to everyone on the earth.'

Still the shepherds don't move. They don't look up. In their fear, they keep their faces hidden; they still try to protect themselves with their hands and arms.

'Something wonderful has happened in Bethlehem.'

The angel goes on. 'The Saviour of the world has been born. The Son of God! One day, because of Him, people will be forgiven for all the wrong things they've done that have broken their friendship with God. One day, they'll be able to live with God forever! Go to Bethlehem now!' the angel cries. 'Go and see Him for yourselves! You'll find Him there, wrapped up safe and warm – but not in a house. Not lying in cradle. The baby is asleep in a manger, tucked away in a stable. Go! Look for Him!'

There's a moment of quiet.

No one moves. Not Topz, not the shepherds. Only Lydia's father risks a cautious peek.

As he slowly raises his head to see the angel floating over him, the singing starts, faintly at first. So faint it's almost impossible to tell where it's coming from. But the sound grows – louder and louder – and, as it does, the sky suddenly flares with the most dazzling brilliance!

Sarah sees Lydia's father nudge his companions; she sees all the shepherds now, still crouched down, but staring upwards, open-mouthed.

THERE ISN'T JUST ONE ANGEL ANYMORE. THE WHOLE OF THE NIGHT SKY IS FILLED WITH THEM. A HUGE ARMY OF ANGELS. HUNDREDS, EVEN THOUSANDS!

The light is blinding, and the sound of singing is like the freest of running rivers and the most explosive of thunder!

'Glory to God in the heights of the heavens and peace to all people on the earth!'

The song echoes round the hills and vibrates on the air. Over and over the words are sung out and carry across the valley.

Until, at last, the light starts to dim, and the singing to fade. And the angels vanish again into darkness.

Lydia runs to her father. His arms close around her.

'What just happened?' he whispers. 'What did we just see?'

One of the other shepherds starts to laugh. 'Would

you believe it?' he chuckles. 'I'm glad you all saw it too, because no one else is *ever* going to believe it!'

'Are we going?' says another. 'Are we going to Bethlehem to find this baby?'

'Well, of course we're going!' splutters Lydia's father. 'Do you think I'm going to just sit here and do nothing when the Son of God's been born? I never imagined something like this happening to me in the whole of my life!'

The laughing shepherd pulls himself together. 'I wonder which stable we're looking for. I suppose we'll have to search all of them.'

Lydia shakes her head. 'No, you won't,' she says. 'I know exactly where the baby is.'

She and the Topz Gang start to lead the shepherds up the hill and out of the valley.

At the ridge, Sarah turns to look back. She can still see the glow of the campfire, and imagines she can still feel its warmth. Otherwise everything lies in darkness.

But overhead, the brightest star in the sky still glistens, while others, tiny and scattered and distant, twinkle with their lower light.

Mary has had her baby. Jesus is born! It's a perfect night. Perfect and clear and extraordinary.

Perfect except for one thing.

Sarah's eyes drift to the star. 'If only John and Gruff and Danny were here. I wish they'd seen all this too...'

CHAPTER 19
Eyes Up
(Isaiah 52 v 7)

'I still think we should have told them.'

John hurries along at Danny's side. Gruff bounds up and down in front of him. Excitement bubbles through every leap. Excitement and joy at being reunited with John, rescued from the palace kitchen yard and, finally, let loose from the basket.

He's not completely free, though. John has untied the belt from his tunic and looped one end through his dog's collar. He holds tightly to the other. It's not that he doesn't trust Gruff – it's just that right now, he doesn't trust anyone else.

'We should have told them,' John says again. 'If we'd told those men King Herod wants to kill the baby, we wouldn't be panicking about trying to find Him before *they* do. They'd know not to go back to Jerusalem.'

Danny's feet pound rhythmically across the rough ground. His walk is almost a jog.

'But we don't know that, do we? Not for sure. For one thing, they might not have believed us. It sounds like King Herod was as nice as pie to them. He probably didn't come over as some sort of mad, jealous baby-hater. And for another, maybe they wouldn't care what King Herod does to the baby. Maybe they think they're friends with royalty now and they'll want to suck up to him. So they'll find Jesus, then go straight back to Jerusalem and tell the king where He is.'

'But they've come all this way to see Jesus!' argues John. 'They want to worship Him. They told King Herod they've got gifts for Him. Why would they bother with any of that if they're not convinced of how special He is?'

Danny shakes his head. 'It's too risky, John. No.' He ups his pace. 'No, we need to get to Bethlehem before they do. We need to find Mary and Joseph and tell them what King Herod said. Tell them they have to leave.'

John gives up. Danny's made up his mind, and there's no changing it.

That's when another thought strikes him.

'Fine,' he huffs. He's breathless from trying to keep up, even with the advantage of Gruff. The little dog bouncing in front of him helps to pull him along. 'But what about when we get there, Danny? We don't know where they're staying in Bethlehem. It could take us ages to track them down. Even if we reach the town first, those three men might find them before we do anyway.'

Danny stops suddenly – so suddenly that Gruff and John carry on for several paces before they realise.

He points. Not forward, but upwards into the sky ahead of them. As the brightness of the day has slipped into the deep blue-black of evening, a few sparks of starlight have begun to appear. Barely noticeable.

But gleaming in the sky with them is another star. It's big and beaming and bold. The star the three men were following. It has to be!

Danny's star.

'If that star led those men all the way to Jerusalem,' he says, 'it's going to lead them all the way to Mary and Joseph and the new baby in Bethlehem.'

John wrinkles his nose. 'So?'

'So, if it can lead them – it can lead us too!'

As suddenly as he stopped, Danny is off again.

'How fast can camels go?' John says. 'Can they go faster than we can? They've got four legs, they're bound to be faster than we are. If they can go faster than us, Danny, those men could overtake us at any minute.'

'They might not have left Jerusalem yet,' says Danny. He won't think like that. He *can't* think like that. 'Maybe they stopped for something to eat. Just keep walking.'

John groans. 'But how much further, Danny?'

'I don't know! Just keep walking and keep your eyes on the sky.'

It's watching the sky that, a short while later, makes them stop again.

Far ahead, at least to the horizon, the darkness flares with radiant light. An unmissable dome of brilliance. Even the star pales against it.

There's a sound. Distant, muffled, rising and falling on the night air.

The boys strain to hear.

'IS THAT... IS THAT SINGING?' Danny murmurs.

Gruff cocks his head to one side, ears pricked. John listens hard but can't make it out.

As they gaze and watch the light finally dissolve, the sound melts away with it.

'Uh...' John frowns into the blackness. 'What just happened?'

Danny is walking again, only much faster like before. How can he answer? All he knows is this night is unlike any night there has ever been before. Any night there will ever be again.

It's God's night.

CHAPTER 20
Real
(Luke 2 v 16–20)

Am I dreaming, God?

Sarah sits a little apart from the rest of the Gang. They've waved goodbye to the shepherds – those ordinary, hard-working men who have just shared this astonishing moment. Nothing will ever compare to this night; to what they've heard and what they've seen.

Lydia has stayed with the Gang. They hang about now on the road into Bethlehem. They don't want to sleep until John and Danny get back.

And Gruff. Of course Gruff will be with them. He just has to be. It might be soon. It may not be till morning, but he'll be there. The boys will have found him, rescued him… won't they?

Sarah holds on to Saucy and prays silently.

If anyone told me about this night, I'd think they were dreaming. If anyone told me they'd seen a sky full of angels and heard them singing, I'd think it was all in their heads. If a shepherd said an angel had invited him to meet the new-born baby Jesus – the Son of God, the Saviour of the world! – I'd say, 'That never happened!

How can that have happened?'

If he described to me the rickety old stable, lit by a dingy lantern, with heaps of straw, and animals watching over a baby king in a manger… I'd think, 'Wow! What an imagination…'

But this isn't a dream, is it, God? And I can't be dreaming it. Because this isn't a story made up in someone's head; a picture a shepherd has created in his mind to make the night pass more quickly.

THIS IS REAL. THIS IS YOUR PLAN. Your Son has been born to Mary, but not in a place fit for a king – in a tiny stable in Bethlehem. Mary wrapped Him up in pieces of cloth and laid Him down to sleep in the animals' feeding trough.

I saw Jesus.

We stayed outside the door when the shepherds went in. Topz and me. We peeped through the gap where they left it open; where the lantern light seeped out.

Mary was there, and Joseph. And the shepherds gathered round the manger. Mary looked surprised to see them. How did they know? Who told them? Why would anyone think they'd find a baby in a stable?

Then the shepherds explained how an angel had invited them. How, out of all the people You could have invited to be the first to meet Your new Son, You chose them. Humble shepherds. In their old clothes and still smelling of the hills and the sheep and the smoke from the campfire. The stew, too, probably.

How the good news of Jesus is for everyone. Every single person living on the planet. Not just the rich and *the powerful, but the poor and the weak; the simple and the ordinary. The shepherds knew that because You chose to tell them first.*

And I stood and I gazed. And in the dim, yellow light, Your baby Son's face seemed to me to shine. Gently breathing. Peacefully sleeping. Does He know that His birth – His arrival here on earth – has changed the world forever?

Then didn't the shepherds praise You, God! Didn't they laugh and sing and stretch their arms out to You as they left Bethlehem behind and went back to their sheep! How we all laughed and sang and praised You!

Sarah breaks off. Her eyes travel skywards and rest on the star. It burns silently and full of the promise of Jesus.

Everything is quiet again now, God. A quiet like I've never known. The air is still. Nothing moves. As if nothing in all the universe wants to disturb the sleeping baby in the stable.

What a gift, Lord God! Knowing Jesus will be the same as knowing You. Not in a dream. Not just in our minds. But in reality. To believe that Jesus is Your Son will be to have life. Life with You forever.

Thank You.

CHAPTER 21

Holy

(Matthew 2 v 9–11)

'Danny! Look, it's Danny!' Sarah's shrieks pierce the silence. 'It's Danny and John and – GRUFF!'

The two boys approach through the darkness. Danny runs. John lags behind, until he realises the Gang are on the road ahead, waiting for them. Then he breaks into a run too, led by Gruff, who strains at the tunic-belt lead. His short legs pelt backwards and forwards like little pistons, propelling him along.

'You're here!'

'You're back!'

'Where was he?'

'You found him!'

'I never thought we'd see him again!'

The cries and questions ring out, one after the other, after the other.

'And guess what?' says Benny. The grin on his face can't stretch any wider. 'Mary's had her baby.'

Danny's face falls. 'Oh, no!'

Benny's eyes narrow in confusion. 'That's not the reaction we were expecting… Why aren't you happy?'

'You don't understand.' Danny starts to pace up and down. He's starving and exhausted, but his body won't keep still. 'If the baby's been born, then He's in danger. Real, proper danger.'

'What danger?' says Josie. 'What are you talking about?'

'KING HEROD WANTS HIM DEAD!' Danny blurts it out. His words hit the air like a shock wave.

'*What?*' Sarah's voice is small and frightened.

Danny tells them about the men – the three visitors to the palace in Jerusalem who know about the birth of a new king because of the star – the huge star he spotted himself a few days before.

It's there even now, shining in the skies over Bethlehem.

'If they find Jesus,' he says, 'they'll go back to King Herod and tell him where He is. King Herod doesn't want another king, so he'll get rid of Him. You have to take me to Him. I have to tell Mary and Joseph that they need to pack up and leave right now!'

Dave stares at him. He doesn't look scared or even angry. He seems puzzled. 'How do you know King Herod wants to kill Jesus? Who told you?'

'A woman who works in the palace kitchen,' John says. 'She helped us get Gruff out. She told us. She heard King Herod say it.'

Sarah's face is white. 'Then we have to go back to the stable. We have to let Mary know. What will they do? She'll be scared to death.'

'No, no wait a minute.' Dave shakes his head.

'We haven't got time to wait!' Danny rounds on him.

'We need to go now. Those men could be right behind us. All they've got to do is follow the star and they'll find Jesus.'

John looks at Sarah. 'Did you say "stable"? What are they doing in a stable?'

Dave ignores him. 'Danny.' His voice is insistent. 'You said those men knew about Jesus because of a star. That star right there.' He points to the sky, but his eyes stay fixed on Danny.

'We're wasting time, Dave!' Danny throws up his hands.

'We were out in the hills earlier with some shepherds. Suddenly, out of nowhere, there was an angel in the sky. The angel told them about a new baby and invited them to go and see Him. The angel came from God – just like the angel who visited Mary.'

'So?' Danny looks desperate.

'So,' Dave says, 'if God sent an angel to tell some shepherds where His Son is, don't you think He put that star in the sky to tell those men the same thing?'

Danny starts to speak – then stops.

'And if God wants those men to visit His Son like the shepherds,' says Dave, 'do you really think He's going to let them tell some king where the baby is so the king can kill Him...?'

* * *

The dingy-yellow lantern light still escapes through the crack where the stable door hangs slightly open.

Mary must be longing for sleep. Does she even want more visitors?

The three men are there. The star showed them the way. It had stopped above the stable – exactly over the ramshackle roof that lets in the rain and creaks when the wind blows. They climb down from their camels, gather together their gifts, and tie up their animals outside.

If they're surprised to find the new king asleep in a manger, they don't show it. To them, it's another part of their extraordinary journey, all the way from their homeland, following a star to Bethlehem. How could anything possibly be normal or as expected after that?

Topz huddle together close to the stable door. The camels stand near them, their eyelids drooping. One creature sags slightly at the knees, then gives up with standing altogether. It collapses to the ground with a grunt and drifts into sleep.

'They're giving their presents,' whispers Danny. He can just about see through the gap. 'I wonder what presents you give to the Son of God?'

Strange presents. Wonderful presents. Another piece of this wondrous night, never to be forgotten.

One visitor gives gold. 'A gift fit for a king,' he says.

Mary smiles. The gleam of the gold under the lantern light reflects in her tired eyes.

The second offers frankincense. 'A gift for God's Son. Your baby will be worshipped on earth and in heaven,' the man says to Mary.

The third places his present in the straw at the foot of the manger. 'And I bring myrrh.' There's a kindness in his face. But a sadness lies there too.

Mary watches the man.

'Myrrh is for this child's life.' His voice is quiet. Gentle. 'This life is more special than any child that has been born before, or will ever be born again. This life will be holy until the very last breath...'

CHAPTER 22
Adventurers
(Matthew 2 v 13–15)

The sun floats just above the horizon, where it shimmers with pink and crimson-gold.

But, to Danny, it's as if the whole morning shines.

He's not afraid anymore. Gruff is safe and the Gang are back together. And Mary and Joseph and their new baby are in God's hands. Held securely and protected.

Danny knows that now for sure.

Whether the three men had taken a nap in Jerusalem before setting off for Bethlehem, or whether they'd stopped and made camp at some point along the road, God had told them in a dream not to go back to King Herod. Not on any account were they to tell King Herod where Jesus was.

So, very early, before daylight, the men had left the stable and the packed little town where Jesus was born. They'd set off on the journey back to their homeland on a different road – one that bypassed Jerusalem.

King Herod could wait for them. He could pace the floor and post guards on the palace roof to look out for them. He could send out a search party.

But he'd never see them again.

Jesus was a baby king he would never find.

GOD WAS IN CONTROL.

Topz had spent what was left of the night at Lydia's house. They'd slept on the floor. Lydia's mum had found all the covers for them she could.

'I'm sorry, it's all I've got,' she'd said. 'Not enough to keep you warm. Not properly. Not on a nippy night like this.'

But even the cold couldn't keep the Gang awake. They were exhausted. From travelling, from fear. From excitement and wonder.

Even Danny, whose head whirled with a hundred thoughts and questions, had fallen asleep almost at once.

At sunrise, though, he is first up.

A finger of pale dawn light reaches in through the window and he opens his eyes. Instantly, he's wide awake. He stretches, and runs his hands through his dusty hair. He rolls over.

His friends are still asleep – fast asleep. Even Gruff and Saucy look lost in the deepest of dreams.

Danny slips out from underneath his thin blanket. Carefully, quietly, he steps over the sleeping Gang. He creeps to the front door and slips through to the street outside.

It's so still; full of shadow under the low sun. Is he the only one awake?

No. He's sure that Mary won't have slept at all. Or Joseph. How could anyone sleep with the Saviour of the world tucked up beside them?

Danny straightens his tunic, rumpled from his few

hours' rest. He stretches again. He yawns and shakes himself down.

Then, 'Father God,' he murmurs. 'What a night… What a totally unbelievable, incredibly amazing night…'

He walks down the street, past the sleeping houses all the way to the edge of the town.

As the road peters out and merges with the plains and hills beyond, he stops. He glances towards the sky.

The stars have vanished. The slowly climbing sun has already chased away their brightness.

The huge star – the leading star – is gone now too. Gone away with the angels. They've all done their job. They've made their announcements and traced the path for God's chosen visitors. The way to the new King – God's gift to the world.

Now a fresh light shines across the earth. The light of Jesus.

In the early morning, with wide open space in front of him and the town clustered behind, Danny prays.

God, You are the Lord of adventure! Powerful and mighty! And we're Your adventurers.

You see everything, God. You hear everything. You know everything because You hold the world in Your hands. You saw it before You'd even created it and You see it now – and right through to the very ending of the universe.

Your love for every single one of us on the earth is so huge that You've sent Your Son here to live with us. To share His days with us. And getting to know Him will be getting to know You too. Because You are in Him.

You are in that tiny baby in the stable. You've come down from heaven to live with the people You've made.

I'm sorry I doubted You, God. I'm sorry I didn't believe You had it all under control. I knew King Herod was out to kill Jesus. I panicked. I thought it was up to us to make sure Herod never found Him. I thought we were the ones who'd have to save Him!

BUT JESUS IS YOUR PLAN TO SAVE THE WORLD *– to bring everyone back to You to be friends with You again. He's been Your plan all along. You've just been waiting for the right time. The perfect time. How could I ever have thought it would all come to nothing because of one mean, jealous, grumpy king?*

God, You are Lord of the universe. Stronger and more powerful and more knowing and understanding than anyone.

Thank You.

There's a hint of warmth to the sun. It's only faint, but Danny can feel it on his back now.

He looks up and stretches his arms towards the sky, just as he does when he's reaching for stars.

He stands there for a long time.

This time he's reaching for God.

*   *   *

'Danny!'

Danny hears John's voice before he sees him.

'What's up?' he says.

Gruff is there. He scampers towards Danny. He lifts

his head and twitches his nose as the scents of the open countryside drift along the air.

'What's up with you?' John asks. 'Still reaching for stars?' He glances upwards. 'Well, you're wasting your time. There aren't any.'

Danny grins. 'Oh, they're there all right. We just can't see them.'

'Anyway, we've got to go,' says John.

'Where? Back to Nazareth? Are Mary and Joseph going home?'

'No. Too dangerous.' John shakes his head. 'King Herod won't give up searching for Jesus. Mary and Joseph have to take Him right away. To Egypt.'

'*Egypt*? But why? God won't let anything happen to them. We know that. He'll look after them.'

'Yes, He will,' says John. 'He is. That's why He sent an angel to Joseph in the night – to tell him they need to get out of Bethlehem and go to Egypt. Egypt is where God will take care of them till it's safe for them to go home.'

Danny nods his head slowly, taking it in.

'So,' says John, 'off we go again. Looks like

THE ADVENTURE'S NOT OVER YET.'

'Over?' Danny looks at his friend; looks once more up towards the sky. 'No, it's definitely not over, John. I'd say it's only just begun.'

'A child is born to us! A son is given to us! And he will be our ruler. He will be called, "Wonderful Counsellor", "Mighty God", "Eternal Father", "Prince of Peace".' (Isaiah 9 v 6)

TOPZ EVERY DAY

Topz is an exciting, day-by-day look at the Bible with the Topz Gang! Full of fun activities, cartoons, prayers and daily Bible readings – dive in and get to know God and His Word!

Available as an annual subscription or as single issues. Find out more at **www.cwr.org.uk/topzeveryday**

MORE TOPZ

There are four different series of *Topz* books for you to discover! Find out more at **www.cwr.org.uk/topzbooks**